from ancient India

ONCE A MOUSE ...

a fable cut in wood

by MARCIA BROWN

ALADDIN BOOKS

MACMILLAN PUBLISHING COMPANY • NEW YORK

COLLIER MACMILLAN PUBLISHERS • LONDON

TO HILDA

Aladdin Books
Macmillan Publishing Company
866 Third Avenue, New York, NY 10022
Collier Macmillan Canada, Inc.
First Aladdin Books edition 1982
Second Aladdin Books edition 1989
Printed in the United States of America
A hardcover edition of *Once a Mouse...* is available from
Charles Scribner's Sons, Macmillan Publishing Company.

10 9 8 7 6 5 4 3

Library of Congress Cataloging-in-Publication Data
Brown, Marcia.
Once a mouse—.
Originally published in 1961 by Scribner.
Summary: As it changes from mouse to cat to dog
to tiger, a hermit's pet also becomes increasingly vain.
1. Fables. 2. Folklore—India. I. Title.
PZ8.2.B668 on 1989   398.24′52   89-32057
ISBN 0-689-71343-6
9780689713439

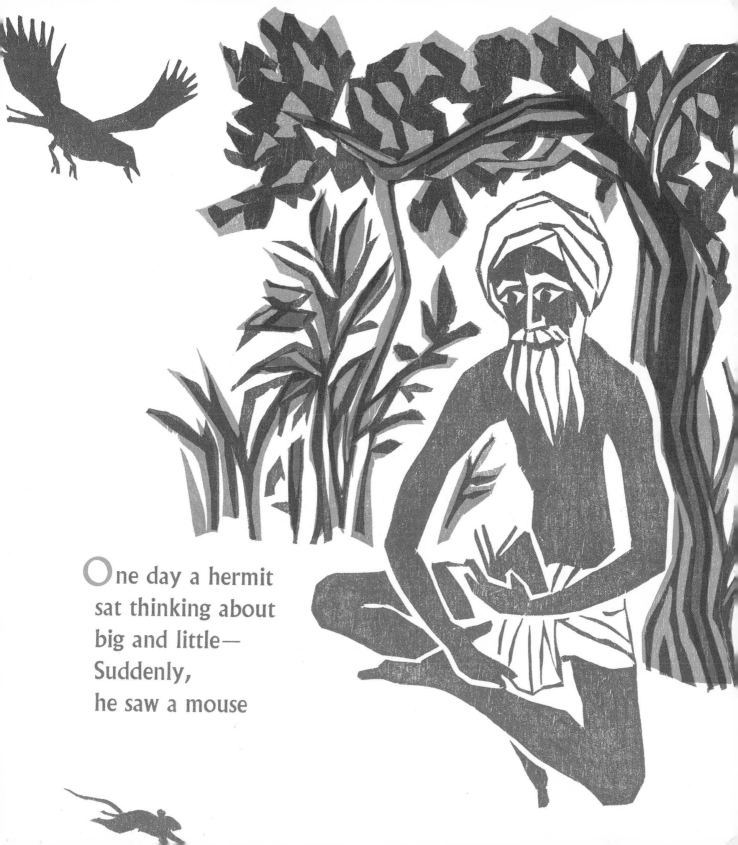

One day a hermit
sat thinking about
big and little—
Suddenly,
he saw a mouse

about to be snatched up by a crow.

He hurried

to help the poor little animal, and tearing him
from the crow's greedy beak, he carried him off to

his hut in the forest, where he comforted him
with milk and grains of rice. But look!

A cat came to the hut with whiskers

straight and tail held high.

But the hermit was mighty at magic as well as at prayer. When he saw the danger threatening his little pet, he quickly changed him into a stout cat. But ...

that night a dog barked in the forest.
Poor puss ran to hide under the bed. The
hermit wasted no time in thinking about
how big or so big, and

changed the cat into a big dog. Not long after that,
a hungry tiger

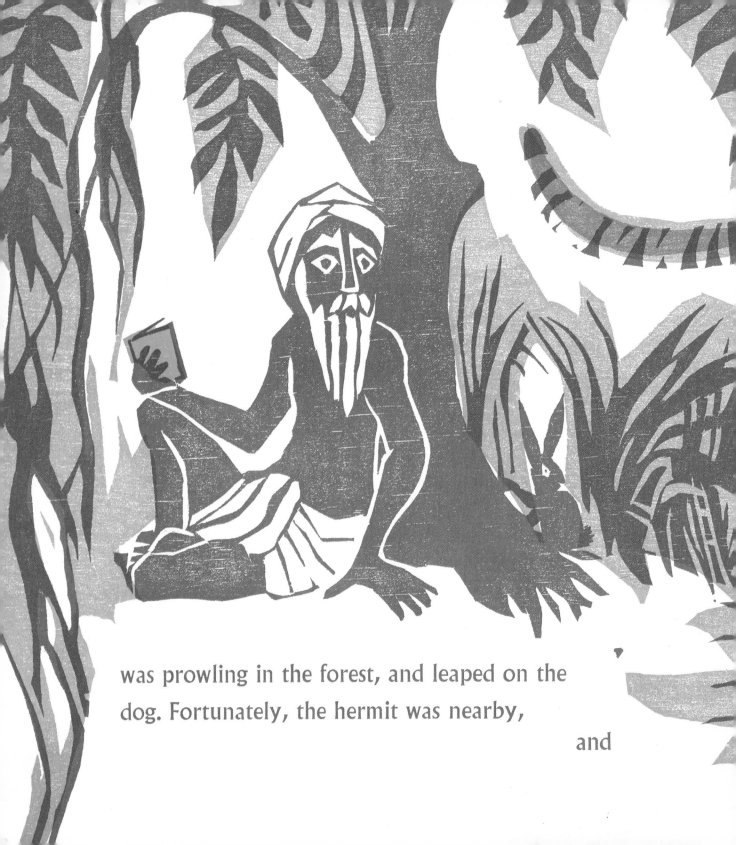

was prowling in the forest, and leaped on the
dog. Fortunately, the hermit was nearby,

and

with a gesture, he changed the dog

into a handsome, royal tiger. Now,

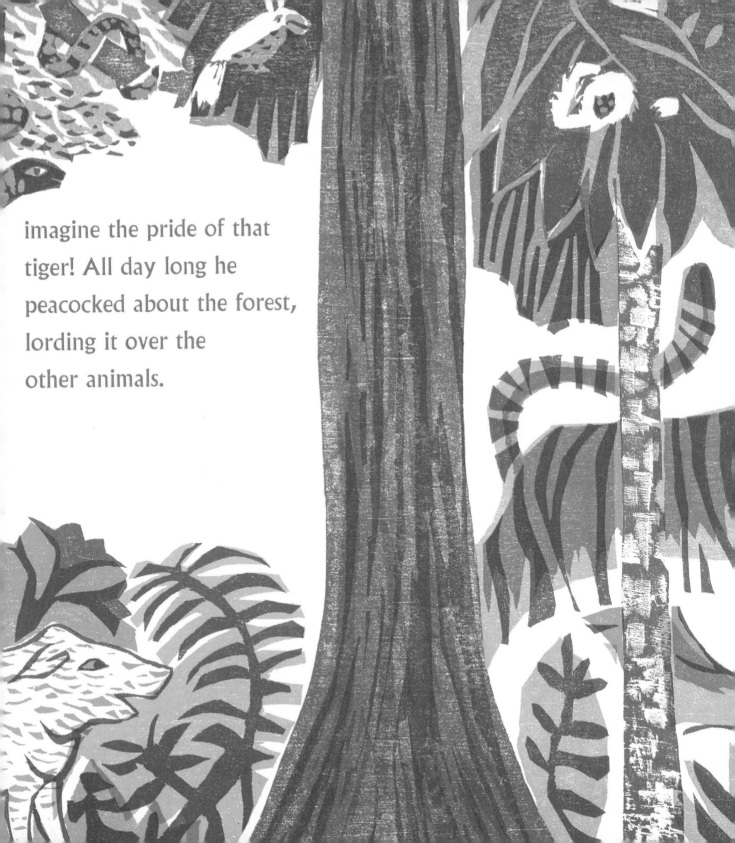

imagine the pride of that
tiger! All day long he
peacocked about the forest,
lording it over the
other animals.

The hermit missed nothing of all this, and chided the beast. "Without me," he would say to him, "you would be a wretched little mouse, that is, if you were still alive. There is no need to give yourself such airs."

The tiger felt offended and humiliated. He forgot
all the good he had received from the old man.

"No one shall tell me that I was once a mouse. I will kill him!"

But the hermit read the tiger's mind.
"You are ungrateful! Go back to the forest and
be a mouse again!"
So the proud and handsome tiger turned back
into a frightened, humble, little mouse

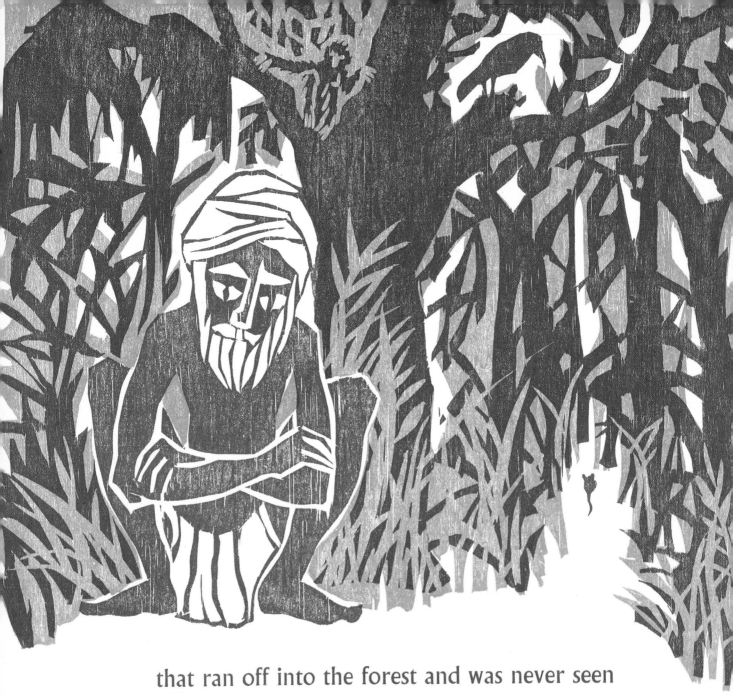

that ran off into the forest and was never seen
again. And the hermit sat thinking about big—
and little . . .